The Little Drummer Boy

The Little

Viking
Published by the Penguin Group
Penguin Putnam Books for Young Readers, 345 Hudson Street, New York,
New York 10014, U.S.A.

Penguin Books Ltd, Registered Offices: Harmondsworth, Middlesex, England

First published in the United States of America in 1968 by the Macmillan Company

Published in 2000 by Viking and Puffin Books,
divisions of Penguin Putnam Books for Young Readers

10 9 8 7 6 5 4 3 2
Copyright © Ezra Jack Keats, 1968
Copyright assigned to Ezra Jack Keats Foundation, 1996
All rights reserved
The Little Drummer Boy words and music by Katherine Davis, Henry Onorati, and
Harry Simeone
© 1958 (renewed 1986) Emi Mills Music, Inc., and International Korwin Corp.
Worldwide print rights on behalf of Emi Mills Music, Inc., administered by Warner
Bros. Publications US Inc.

LIBRARY OF CONGRESS CATALOGING-IN-PUBLICATION DATA
Keats, Ezra Jack.
The little drummer boy / Ezra Jack Keats ; words and music by
Katherine Davis, Henry Onorati and Harry Simeone.
p. cm.
Originally published: The little drummer boy / Katherine Davis.
New York: Macmillan, 1968.
Summary: An illustrated version of the Christmas carol about the
procession to Bethlehem and the offer of a poor boy to play his drum for
the Christ Child.
ISBN 0-670-89226-2 (hardcover) — ISBN 0-14-056743-7 (pbk.)
1. Carols, English—Texts. 2. Christmas music—Texts. [1. Carols. 2.
Christmas music.] I. Davis, Katherine, 1892- II. Onorati, Henry.
III. Simeone, Harry. IV. Davis, Katherine, 1892- Little drummer boy. V. Title.
PZ8.3.K227 Li 2000
782.42'1723—dc21 00-008665

Printed in Hong Kong

Drummer Boy

EZRA JACK KEATS

Words and Music by Katherine Davis,
Henry Onorati and Harry Simeone

VIKING

Come, they told me,
(pa-rum-pum-pum-pum)

Our newborn King to see,
(pa-rum-pum-pum-pum)

Our finest gifts to bring
(pa-rum-pum-pum-pum)

To lay before the King,
(pa-rum-pum-pum-pum, rum-pum-pum-pum, rum-pum-pum-pum)

So to honor Him
(*pa-rum-pum-pum-pum*)

When we come.

Baby Jesus,
(pa-rum-pum-pum-pum)

I am a poor boy too,
(*pa-rum-pum-pum-pum*)

I have no gift to bring
(pa-rum-pum-pum-pum)

That's fit to give a king,
(pa-rum-pum-pum-pum,
rum-pum-pum-pum,
rum-pum-pum-pum)

Shall I play for you
(*pa-rum-pum-pum-pum*)

On my drum?

I played my best for Him,
*(pa-rum-pum-pum-pum,
rum-pum-pum-pum,
rum-pum-pum-pum)*

I played my drum for Him,
(pa-rum-pum-pum-pum)

The ox and lamb kept time,
(*pa-rum-pum-pum-pum*)

Mary nodded,
(pa-rum-pum-pum-pum)

Then He smiled at me,
(pa-rum-pum-pum-pum)

Me and my drum.

The Little Drummer Boy

Words and Music by KATHERINE DAVIS, HENRY ONORATI and HARRY SIMEONE

MODERATO

Come, they told me, pa-rum pum pum pum — Our new-born

King to see, pa-rum pum pum pum — Our fin-est gifts to bring, pa-

rum pum pum pum — To lay be-fore the King, pa-rum pum pum pum,

rum pum pum pum, rum pum pum pum — So to hon-our Him, pa-

rum pum pum pum — When — we come. —

Mar - y nod-ded, pa-rum pum pum pum — The Ox and

Lamb kept time, pa-rum pum pum pum — I played my drum for Him, pa-

rum pum pum pum — I played my best for Him, pa - rum pum pum pum,

rum pum pum pum, rum pum pum pum — Then He smiled at me, pa-

rum pum pum pum — Me and my drum. —